Why Do You Love Me?

For
Theo Little
and Theo Big

Copyright © 1988 by Martin Baynton
First published in New Zealand in 1989 by Ashton Scholastic Limited
First published in the United States in 1990 by Greenwillow Books
All rights reserved. No part of this book may be reproduced
or utilized in any form or by any means, electronic or mechanical,
including photocopying, recording or by any information storage and
retrieval system, without permission in writing from the Publisher,
Greenwillow Books, a division of William Morrow & Company, Inc.,
105 Madison Avenue, New York, N.Y. 10016.
Printed in Hong Kong   First Edition   10 9 8 7 6 5 4 3 2 1

Library of Congress Cataloging-in-Publication Data
Baynton, Martin.
Why do you love me? / Martin Baynton.   p.   cm.
"First published in New Zealand in 1989 by
Ashton Scholastic Limited" CIP t.p. verso.
Summary: A father and son share a special time together walking
the dog as the boy questions why his father loves him.
ISBN 0-688-09156-3.   ISBN 0-688-09157-1 (lib. bdg.)
[1. Fathers—Fiction.]   I. Title.   PZ7.B347Wh   1990
[E]—dc 19   89-1861   CIP   AC

Why Do You Love Me?

Martin Baynton

GREENWILLOW BOOKS, NEW YORK

Do you love me?

Yes, I love you very much.

Why do you?

Oh, lots of reasons.

Do you love me because I'm strong?

Mmmm, perhaps.

Do you love me because I'm fast?

Yes, and when you're slow too.

And when I'm kind?

Certainly when you're kind . . . oops!

Do you love me when I'm brave?

Yes, but be careful.

And when I'm funny?

Yes, but please, *please* be careful.

Do you love me when I'm clever?

Yes . . . *watch out!*

Do you love me when I'm naughty?

Yes, even when you're naughty.

As much as when I'm good?

Yes, just as much.

Why do I try to be good then?

I don't know why. You tell me.

Because I love you too.

E
BAY   Bayton, Martin

Why do you love me?

$12.95

E BAY	Bayton, Martin	
AUTHOR		
	Why do you love me?	
TITLE		
$12.95		
DATE DUE	BORROWER'S NAME	ROOM NUMBER
1-2	Stefan P.	2D
2/6	Erica W.	2M
10-1	Ashley S.	2K
3-4	D. Mastrocol...	